BETTER THAN YOU

TRUDY LUDWIG

ILLUSTRATED BY **ADAM GUSTAVSON**

ALFRED A. KNOPF 🐎 **NEW YORK**

To Nicole Geiger, Abigail Samoun, and Laura Mancuso.
Thank you for your unwavering support. –TJL

THIS IS A BORZOI BOOK PUBLISHED BY ALFRED A. KNOPF

Text copyright © 2011 by Trudy Jean Ludwig
Jacket art and interior illustrations copyright © 2011 by Adam Gustavson

All rights reserved. Published in the United States by Alfred A. Knopf, an imprint of Random House Children's Books,
a division of Random House, Inc., New York.

Knopf, Borzoi Books, and the colophon are registered trademarks of Random House, Inc.

Visit us on the Web! www.randomhouse.com/kids

Educators and librarians, for a variety of teaching tools, visit us at www.randomhouse.com/teachers

Library of Congress Cataloging-in-Publication Data
Ludwig, Trudy.
Better than you / by Trudy Ludwig ; illustrations by Adam Gustavson. —1st ed.
p.   cm.
Includes bibliography.
Summary: Tyler's friend Jake continually boasts about his abilities, making Tyler feel bad about himself
until his uncle Kevin and new neighbor Niko help him see that Jake is the one with the problem.
ISBN 978-1-58246-380-3 (trade) — ISBN 978-1-58246-407-7 (lib. bdg.)
[1. Pride and vanity—Fiction. 2. Self-esteem—Fiction. 3. Friendship—Fiction. 4. Interpersonal relations—Fiction.] I. Gustavson, Adam, ill. II. Title.
PZ7.L9763Bet 2011
[Fic]—dc22
2010033224

MANUFACTURED IN CHINA
September 2011
10 9 8 7 6 5 4 3 2 1

First Edition

FOREWORD

There's a bad attitude spreading among kids these days and it's got a name: arrogance. No child is born arrogant, yet more kids are bragging about their accomplishments and comparing their possessions and achievements to others'. This disturbing trend, which I attribute in large part to our competitive, materialistic, and "praise-aholic" culture, is not only unbecoming, it also doesn't lead to lasting friendships. The good news is that kids can learn to curb their arrogance, and it's up to the caring adults in their lives to show them how.

Don't get me wrong: I'm not belittling any child's talents or skills. This issue isn't about what a kid can do or how he looks. It's about his preoccupation with being center stage, making sure everyone knows just how great he is. And researchers report that this childhood need to demonstrate competencies, if left unchecked, will remain a pattern in adulthood as well.

A child's sense of self-worth should not be contingent upon earning approval and accolades from others. The best self-esteem is internalized, with the child gaining a sense of pride and inner confidence in accomplishing something for the simple joy of doing it on his own.

When parents ask me for advice on how to change their children's boastful ways, I often recommend these key strategies:

* Uncover the source of the arrogant attitude. Does your daughter feel that she has to get straight A's or win a trophy or award to gain your approval or love? Is your son constantly trying to impress his friends because deep down he feels inadequate? Getting to the root of your child's problem will help you make the necessary changes to find effective solutions.

* Help kids recognize the impact their attitude has on others. Foster empathy and a healthy perspective with role-playing, pointing out nonverbal reactions, and asking how your child would feel if he were in the other person's shoes.

* Focus more on character, not just performance. Do you stress personal accomplishments (grades, athletic strength, awards, etc.) over character traits (kindness, intelligence, patience, etc.)? Help your child to be more understanding and accepting of her own strengths and weaknesses.

* Acknowledge others' accomplishments. Encourage your child to look for the good in others and to make frequent efforts to compliment peers on their particular skills, strengths, or talents.

* Reinforce humility and acts of kindness. Temper boasting and bragging by commending personal displays of humility, kindness, and generosity toward others. Also, remind your child to say thank you after someone compliments him.

After reading *Better than You* by Trudy Ludwig, I'd like to recommend another great strategy: read this book to the kids in your life. I love *Better than You* because it really zeroes in on the fact that absolutely no good comes out of arrogance. What child wants to hang out with someone like Jake, who makes him feel inferior?

Trudy's wonderful story also lets children know that bragging has nothing to do with the kid on the receiving end and everything to do with the kid on the giving end. Readers—both young and old—will easily relate to Tyler's feelings about his friend's constant one-upmanship tactics. And Uncle Kevin's marvelous comparison of Jake to a pufferfish will put a knowing smile on any reader's face.

Better than You cuts right into the heart of arrogance with insight, empathy, and humor. Like Trudy's other books, this is a must-read for generating thoughtful discussion about real friendship issues kids face on a daily basis.

Michele Borba, EdD
Today show contributor
Recipient of the National Educator Award
Author of *The Big Book of Parenting Solutions* and
    Don't Give Me That Attitude!

My neighbor Jake can be a real jerk—always letting me know that whatever I do, he can do better.

Don't get me wrong. Jake is great at practically everything he does—especially sports. Me? Not so much. I mean, I know I'm good at writing stories and playing the guitar, but when it comes to basketball, I have to practice a lot just to be a decent player.

The jerky side of Jake first started to bug me when I was trying to learn how to do a layup. For weeks I'd been working on leaping, aiming, and shooting like an NBA star. I even got my older brother Iggy's help. I was so excited when I could finally do it that I went over to Jake's house to show him.

"Hey, Tyler—what's up?" said Jake.

"Check this out: I can do a layup!"

After I showed him the move, he grabbed the
basketball from me and said, "Yeah, well, I bet you can't
do this. . . ." Then Jake did a perfect hook shot.

He couldn't just say, "Cool, Tyler!" or "Great job—
you nailed it!" Nope. He had to outdo me.

Who am I kidding? I thought. I'll never be great at
basketball. Why even bother trying?

Last Tuesday morning I was in the middle of showing Sharise my new music player when Jake came over.

"What's that?" he asked.

"It's a SoundLaunch," replied Sharise. "Tyler just bought it."

"You're kidding! A SoundLaunch? You should've gotten a Tunage 300," said Jake.

Then he went on and on about all the great things his music player could do that mine couldn't. I just stood there, thinking of all the places I'd rather be than right there with Jake.

Today we had a math test. I hate math. It's my hardest subject. My hands get all sweaty and my brain turns to mush whenever I try to solve the problems. Do you want to know what was worse than taking that test? Having the teacher tell you that the kid to your right would be grading it. And since I sat next to Jake, he got to check my answers.

"Geez, Tyler, I can't believe you got some of these problems wrong," he said. "This test was so-o-o easy. I must be, like, five times smarter than you in math."

There should be a law that kids don't get to grade each other's tests.

Stupid test.

Stupid me.

When I came home from school, I threw down my backpack, headed to my bedroom, and slammed the door.

"Hey, Tyler," called Iggy from downstairs. "Uncle Kevin's here."

When I didn't go say hi to Uncle Kevin, he came upstairs.

"Why are you holed up in your room?" he asked.

I didn't say anything and just kept tossing my basketball up in the air.

"You know, Tyler, one of my favorite ways to get rid of the blues is to play 'em," he told me.

We went out to the front porch and started strumming away. Uncle Kevin was right. Playing the guitar did help me feel better. But it still didn't solve my problem with Jake.

After a while, Uncle Kevin asked, "Did you have a tough day at school?"

"More like a tough month," I grumbled. "My friend Jake's been getting on my nerves a lot lately. I know he's better than me at a bunch of stuff, but he doesn't have to rub it in my face all the time. I feel like such a loser when I'm around him."

Uncle Kevin nodded as he strummed some more chords. "Is Jake like this around your other friends, too?"

I thought about it for a minute. I remembered hearing Carlos tell Oscar at baseball practice that he was sick of Jake's bragging. "He thinks he's better than us," said Carlos.

"Yeah. What a show-off!" agreed Oscar.

So it wasn't only me that Jake treated this way. The other guys were getting fed up with him, too. Maybe it wasn't my fault after all. Maybe it had more to do with him than with me.

I shared this with Uncle Kevin, and he told me that people like Jake are a lot like the pufferfish we saw at the aquarium last summer. They puff up their bodies to make themselves bigger than they actually are.

"It's a way of protecting themselves from potential enemies," he explained. "But when a kid acts like a pufferfish, he takes up so much space that he can also push away friends."

Uncle Kevin suddenly stood up and shouted, "Make way for Pufferfish Man!" as he chased me around the porch.

Mom almost had a heart attack when she came face to face with Pufferfish Man. I laughed so hard my sides were hurting.

After Uncle Kevin left, I biked to the schoolyard. When I
got there, Jake and Niko, this new kid on my street, were on
the field, throwing a Frisbee.

"Hey," I said, nodding in their direction. "Can I play, too?"

"Sure," they both said.

When it was my turn to throw the Frisbee, I flicked
my wrist and put a sweet spin on the disk, flinging it
directly to Niko.

"Nice!" said Niko.

"Thanks," I replied.

And then Jake did what he does best: he puffed up.
"That's nothing," he said. "Look what I can do."

When it was Niko's turn, he did this amazing throw. Our eyes nearly popped out of our heads.

"Wow! That was awesome!" I told Niko.

"Thanks. I could teach you how to do it."

"Really?"

"Sure . . . only if you show me how you did your throw."

"You bet!"

Then Niko turned to Jake. "I can show you, too, if you'd like."

"Yeah, well, I know all the cool Frisbee throws I need to know," said Jake as he started walking off the field.

I ran up to him and said, "C'mon, Jake, don't go. So what if Niko throws better than us? He's cool. Let's just toss the Frisbee around. It'll be fun."

"Nah, I'm out of here. You coming?"

I looked at Jake and then at Niko. "No thanks. I'm going to stay here with Niko."

"Whatever," muttered Jake as he turned and headed home by himself.

Niko and I took turns teaching each other different throws and ended up talking about all kinds of stuff. I found out that Niko just got a guitar for his birthday, so I offered to teach him to play. He thought that was a great idea. You know what? I have a feeling that Niko and I are going to be really good friends.

Author's Note About Bragging and Boasting

In my travels throughout the U.S., many parents, educators, and school counselors have expressed to me their growing concerns with the "I'm better than you" attitude among children these days. While there is nothing wrong with a child feeling pride and a sense of accomplishment in his or her abilities, there is definitely something wrong with expressing these feelings in ways that are demeaning to others.

As character-education expert Dr. Michele Borba points out in her book *Don't Give Me That Attitude!,* "Arrogant children's methods of letting others in on their superiority are usually quite tactless and always insensitive. After all, these children dwell on their own capabilities and are usually quite blind to those of others."

Experts list numerous reasons for a child's boastful behavior: self-centeredness; jealousy; feelings of inadequacy or insecurity; over-the-top parental praise of a child's talents and skills; a need to prove oneself to gain parental attention, acceptance, and love; and an environment of one-upmanship when it comes to sports, grades, social status, and materialism.

Regardless of the cause, bragging, boasting, or crowing is not the way to make and keep friends. Nobody likes to feel inferior. And kids who act superior lead lonely social lives.

When children run up against braggarts and boasters (and it's inevitable they will), remind them of Uncle Kevin's observation: kids with puffed-up opinions of themselves "take up so much space that they can push away friends." Your children will have happier, healthier relationships when they learn to gravitate toward friends who can accept all the goodness they have to offer and give it back in kind.

Below are some suggestions to help children turn painful encounters into positive life lessons:

* Know that the other kid's "better than you" attitude has nothing to do with you. It's not your fault.

* Hang out with kids who appreciate and like you for who you are.

* Choose friends who make you feel accepted and safe.

* Nobody is great at everything he or she does. Be more accepting of your strengths and weaknesses, as well as those of others.

* Treat your friends the way you want to be treated—with kindness, compassion, and respect.

For more information on how to help children thrive in their social world, refer to "Recommended Books for Adults" on page 32.

Trudy Ludwig

Questions for Discussion

"My neighbor Jake can be a real jerk—always letting me know that whatever I do, he can do better."

What are some specific examples in the story of how Jake shows he's better than Tyler?

Have you ever been around a kid who lets you know he's better than you at something or owns cooler things than you? If yes, how did that make you feel?

Is it okay to be proud of your own accomplishments? Why or why not?

How do you think Jake could have shared his accomplishments or capabilities in ways that aren't insulting to others?

"I feel like such a loser when I'm around him."

What were some of Tyler's strengths in this story? What were some of his weaknesses?

What were some of Jake's strengths?

What were some of his weaknesses?

What do you consider to be *your* strengths? What do you consider to be *your* weaknesses?

Is it possible to become stronger or better at something you're not as good at right now? If yes, how?

"Maybe it wasn't my fault after all. Maybe it had more to do with him than with me."

What made Tyler realize that Jake's bragging and boasting had more to do with Jake than with him?

Uncle Kevin compared Jake to a pufferfish. Do you agree with his description? Why or why not?

Why do you think Tyler had a feeling that he and Niko were going to be really good friends?

What kinds of qualities do you look for in a friend?

Recommended Books for Adults

Borba, Michele, EdD. *The Big Book of Parenting Solutions: 101 Answers to Your Everyday Challenges and Wildest Worries.* San Francisco: Jossey-Bass, 2009.

Borba, Michele, EdD. *Don't Give Me That Attitude! 24 Rude, Selfish, Insensitive Things Kids Do and How to Stop Them.* San Francisco: Jossey-Bass, 2004.

Dweck, Carol S., PhD. *Mindset: The New Psychology of Success.* New York: Random House, 2006.

Guthrie, Elisabeth, MD, and Kathy Matthews. *No More Push Parenting: How to Find Success and Balance in a Hypercompetitive World.* New York: Broadway Books, 2003.

Kindlon, Dan, PhD, and Michael Thompson, PhD. *Raising Cain: Protecting the Emotional Life of Boys.* New York: Ballantine Books, 2000.

Masarie, Kathy, MD, Jody Bellant Scheer, MD, and Kathy Keller Jones, MA. *Raising Our Daughters: The Ultimate Parenting Guide for Healthy Girls and Thriving Families.* Portland: Family Empowerment Network, 2009.

Masarie, Kathy, MD, Jody Bellant Scheer, MD, and Kathy Keller Jones, MA. *Raising Our Sons: The Ultimate Parenting Guide for Healthy Boys and Strong Families.* Portland: Family Empowerment Network, 2009.

Mortola, Peter, PhD, Howard Hiton, LPC, and Stephen Grant, LCSW. *BAM! Boys Advocacy and Mentoring: A Leader's Guide to Facilitating Strengths-Based Groups for Boys.* New York: Routledge, 2007.

Pollack, William, PhD. *Real Boys: Rescuing Our Sons from the Myths of Boyhood.* New York: Owl Books, 1999.

Pollack, William, PhD, and Kathleen Cushman. *Real Boys Workbook: The Definitive Guide to Understanding and Interacting with Boys of All Ages.* New York: Villard, 2001.

Rubin, Kenneth H., PhD, and Andrea Thompson. *The Friendship Factor: Helping Our Children Navigate Their Social World—and Why It Matters for Their Success and Happiness.* New York: Penguin Books, 2003.

Thompson, Michael, PhD, Catherine O'Neill Grace, and Lawrence J. Cohen, PhD. *Best Friends, Worst Enemies: Understanding the Social Lives of Children.* New York: Ballantine Books, 2002.